How to Care for Your T-Rex

Ken Baker

Illustrated by
Dave Coverly

Christy Ottaviano Books
Henry Holt and Company
New York

To Dave and Karen D., thank you for your
extraordinary goodness, love, and family
—K. B.

For my grandparents, Charles and Betty Coverly,
and Ken and Edna Doehring, for passing down humor,
a passion to create, and love
—D. C.

When you take good care of your T-Rex,
your T-Rex will take good care of you.

T-Rex care starts with exercise every morning.
A T-Rex can cover **fifteen feet** in a single step.
So, unless you have a huge yard, you'll need to go
on brisk walks with your T-Rex.

Your T-Rex will eat approximately **300 pounds** of meat a day. That's about the same amount of calories that eighty adults eat.

What an **appetite!** After your walk, you need to make sure your T-Rex has plenty to eat.

Once breakfast is over, you should spend some time teaching your T-Rex good manners.

Lunchtime at the park can be a great adventure

for you, your T-Rex, and all your friends.

A twenty-foot-tall T-Rex makes a great slide.

Wheeeee!

Even when mistakes are made, always treat your T-Rex with kindness. If its feelings get hurt, it might run away. And at speeds of up to twelve miles per hour, your T-Rex will be hard to catch.

Just don't ask your T-Rex to rescue kites from trees. Its **three-foot-long** arms make it harder to reach things than you might think.

But best of all, like many pets, a T-Rex drools a lot when it gets excited. That can be a lifesaver by the end of a hot summer day at the park.

After dinner, you and your T-Rex need to settle down.
That means quiet time, no excitement, and definitely . . .

NO TICKLING!

When it's time to get ready for bed, your T-Rex will need help brushing and flossing its **nine-inch teeth.** It's not that easy with **six-inch claws** and only two fingers on each hand.

The best way to help your T-Rex settle down
for bed is to read it a favorite story.

After being tucked in with its favorite blanket and stuffed animal, every T-Rex wants one last hug.

And to be sure your T-Rex knows you really care, always remember to sing the most-loved T-Rex lullaby of all:

"Sleep tight, little T-Rex, tickles are done.
Playtime is over. We've had lots of fun.
A new day awaits. More antics in sight.
Sleep tight, little T-Rex,
sleep tight
and
good
night."

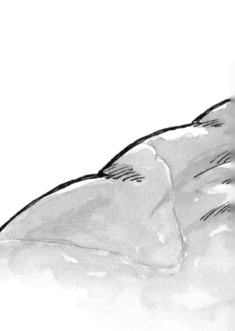

More Fun T-Rex Facts

 T-Rex is short for *Tyrannosaurus rex*, which actually means "tyrant lizard king."

 T-Rex lived about 66 to 68 million years ago, during the Cretaceous period.

 T-Rex made its home in valleys with forests and rivers in what is now known as western North America.

 From head to tail, T-Rex grew to be forty feet long. That's about as long as a school bus.

 Even though T-Rex crouched forward, it would stand up to twenty feet tall. That's more than five times as tall as an average six-year-old kid.

 T-Rex's three-foot-long arms might seem big to us humans, but they were small compared to its long body. Its fingers couldn't even reach its mouth.

 Even though its arms were small, they were strong. Each arm could lift more than 440 pounds.

 With a jaw that was four feet long, T-Rex had a very big mouth.

 T-Rex needed a big mouth to hold its fifty-eight or more cone-shaped, saw-like teeth.

If dinosaurs wore hats, T-Rex would need a big one. Some T-Rex heads were up to five feet long.

With such a big head on one end, T-Rex needed its twenty-foot-long tail on the other to help keep its balance when it stood, walked, and ran.

T-Rex had the best sense of smell of all the meat-eating dinosaurs.

T-Rex had great eyesight, with binocular-like vision wider than a hawk's and sharper than an eagle's.

T-Rex had big feet that were about thirty-nine inches long. However, its footprints were half that size because T-Rex walked on its toes, like most other dinosaurs.

Two of the largest known T-Rex skeletons are named "Sue" and "Stan" after the paleontologists who found them—Sue Hendrickson and Stan Sacrison. A paleontologist is someone who studies fossils. Dinosaur bones are a kind of fossil.

The fossilized bones of both T-Rex Sue and T-Rex Stan were found in South Dakota.

T-Rex Sue is over 90 percent complete, with more than 250 recovered bones and teeth.

Henry Holt and Company, *Publishers since 1866*
Henry Holt® is a registered trademark of Macmillan Publishing Group, LLC
175 Fifth Avenue, New York, NY 10010
mackids.com

Library of Congress Cataloging-in-Publication Data
Names: Baker, Ken, 1962- author. | Coverly, Dave, illustrator.
Title: How to care for your T-Rex / Ken Baker ; illustrated by Dave Coverly.
Description: First edition. | New York : Henry Holt and Company, 2019. |
Summary: How to care for a pet that eats 300 pounds of
meat per day, has tiny arms, and a lot of slobber.
Identifiers: LCCN 2018021021 | ISBN 978-1-250-13751-7 (hardcover)
Subjects: | CYAC: Tyrannosaurus rex—Fiction. | Dinosaurs—Fiction. |
Pets—Fiction.
Classification: LCC PZ7.B17428 Ho 2019 | DDC [E[—dc21
LC record available at https://lccn.loc.gov/20180210217

Our books may be purchased in bulk for promotional, educational, or business use.
Please contact your local bookseller or the Macmillan Corporate and Premium Sales Department
at (800) 221-7945 ext. 5442 or by e-mail at MacmillanSpecialMarkets@macmillan.com.

First edition, 2019
The artist used ink and watercolors on Arches 90-pound hot-press watercolor paper to create the illustrations for this book.
Printed in China by Toppan Leefung Printing Ltd., Dongguan City, Guangdong Province
1 3 5 7 9 10 8 6 4 2